THE EROTIC TEMPLE

AN EROTIC FAIRY TALE

CLOVER'S FANTASY ADVENTURES
BOOK 11

VICTORIA RUSH

VOLUME 11

CLOVER'S FANTASY ADVENTURES -
BOOK 11

COPYRIGHT

ALSO BY VICTORIA RUSH

Adult Fairytales:

The Enchanted Forest: An Erotic Fairytale

The Land of Giants: An Erotic Fairytale

The Dragon's Lair: An Erotic Fairytale

Witch's Brew: An Erotic Fairytale

The Mage's Spell: An Erotic Fairytale

The Mermaid Lagoon: An Erotic Fairytale

The Coven: An Erotic Fairytale

Rapunzel: An Erotic Fairytale

The Seven Dwarfs: An Erotic Fairytale

The Land of Mutants: An Erotic Fairytale

The Erotic Temple: A Sexy Fairytale (Coming Soon)

Erotica Themed Bundles:

Voyeur: Lesbian Erotica Bundle

Public Affairs: A Lesbian Anthology

Futa Fantasies: The Ladyboy Collection

Threesomes: The Lesbian Collection

Threesomes - Volume 2: The Lesbian Collection

First Time: A Lesbian Anthology

Hedonism: An Erotic Anthology

Switch Hitters: Bisexual Erotica

Taboo Erotica: The Lesbian Series

BDSM: The Lesbian Collection

Party Games: The Erotic Collection

Party Games 2: The Erotic Collection

All Girl 1: Lesbian Erotica Bundle

All Girl 2: Lesbian Erotica Bundle

All Girl 3: Lesbian Erotica Bundle

All Girl 4: Lesbian Erotica Bundle

Erotic Fairytale Bundles:

Clover's Fantasy Adventures: Books 1 - 5

Clover's Fantasy Adventures: Books 6 - 10

Erotic Fantasy:

Pirate's Bounty: A Time Travel Adventure

Wild West: A Time Travel Adventure

Private Riley: A Time Travel Adventure

Cleopatra's Secret: A Time Travel Adventure

Bounty Hunter 2125: A Time Travel Adventure

Ninja Assassin: A Time Travel Adventure

The 300: A Time Travel Adventure

Arabian Nights: An Erotic Fairytale (coming soon...)

Steamy Time Travel Bundles:

Riley's Time Travel Adventures: Books 1 - 5

Lesbian Erotica:

The Dinner Party: Lesbian Voyeur Erotica

The Darkroom: Bisexual Voyeur Erotica

Naked Yoga: Lesbian Transgender Erotica

Nude Cruise: Bisexual Voyeur Erotica

Rush Hour: Taboo Public Sex

The Girl Next Door: First Time Lesbian Erotic Romance

Girls' Camp: Lesbian Group Sex

Wet Dream: Ladyboy Fantasy Erotica

The Convent: Taboo Sex with a Nun

Sex Robot: A Dream Sex Machine

The Personal Trainer: Getting Pumped at the Gym

The Dominatrix: BDSM Lesbian Domination

Webcam Chat: Lesbian Online Sex

Paint Me: A Kinky Bodypainting Workshop

The Toy Party: Girls Sharing Sex Toys

The Costume Party: Strapping One On

Swedish Sauna: Lesbian Group Sex

The Therapist: Taboo Lesbian Erotica

Elevator Shaft: Bisexual Threesomes Erotica

Ladyboy: Lesbian Transgender Erotica

Peep Show: Lesbian Voyeur Erotica

The Dare: Public Sex Erotica

Maid Service: Lesbian Threesomes Erotica

The Hitchhiker: First Time Lesbian Erotica

The Housesitter: Spycam Lesbian Erotica

The Spa: Lesbian Group Orgy

Parlor Games: Blindfold Sex Party

The Exchange Student: First Time Lesbian Erotica

The Hostel: Bisexual Group Erotica

The Harem: Lesbian Erotic Romance

The Orient Express: Lesbian Voyeur Erotica

The First Lady: A Forbidden Lesbian Erotic Romance

The Slave: Lesbian BDSM Erotica

The Masseuse: Lesbian Sensuous Erotica

Too Close for Comfort: Lesbian Forbidden Erotica

Naked Twister: A Wild Party Game

Lexi: The Sex App (Lesbian Fantasy Erotica)

Call Girl: Lesbian Bisexual Threesomes Erotica

Circle Jill: Lesbian Masturbation Workshop

The Viewing Room: Masturbation Voyeur Erotica

Spin the Bottle: A Kinky Party Game

The Hair Salon: Lesbian Voyeur Erotica

Tribadism 1: Girls Only Sex Workshop

Tribadism 2: The Art of Scissoring

Tribadism 3: Threeway Hookups

The Kiss: A Game of Oral Sex

Pledge Week: Sorority Sisters

Carny Games 1: A Wild Sex Party

Carny Games 2: A Kinky Sex Party

Carny Games 3: An Erotic Sex Party

Dreamscape: An Artificial Reality Game

Glory Hole: Guess Who's On the Other Side

Joy Ride: A Late Night Erotic Bus Trip

The Blind Girl: An Erotic Romance(Coming Soon)

Lesbian Erotica Bundles:

Jade's Erotic Adventures: Books 1 - 5

Jade's Erotic Adventures: Books 6 - 10

Jade's Erotic Adventures: Books 11 - 15

Jade's Erotic Adventures: Books 16 - 20

Jade's Erotic Adventures: Books 21 - 25

Jade's Erotic Adventures: Books 26 - 30

Jade's Erotic Adventures: Books 31 - 35

Jade's Erotic Adventures: Books 36 - 40

Jade's Erotic Adventures: Books 41 - 45

Jade's Erotic Adventures: Books 46 - 50

Fifty Shades of Jade: Superbundle

Standalone Stories:

The Polynesian Girl: A Lesbian EroticRomance

For the uninhibited...

WANT TO AMP UP YOUR SEX LIFE?

Sign up for my newsletter to receive more free books and other steamy stuff. Discover a hundred different ways to wet your whistle!

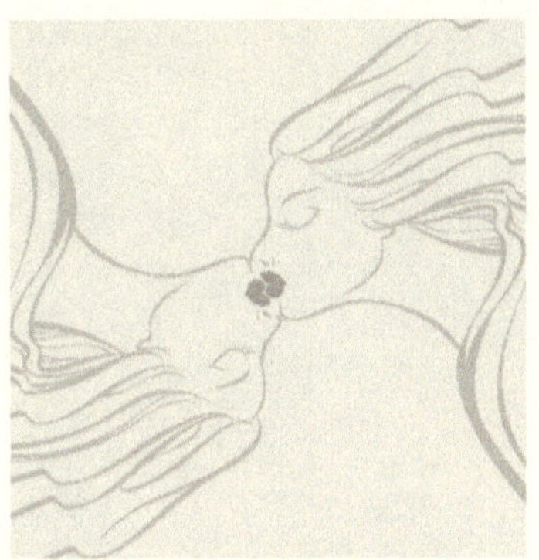

Victoria Rush Erotica

1

After Clover, Tara, and Jessop left the camp of the strange tribespeople with multiple sex organs, they traipsed through the woods, feeling alternately exhausted and elated.

"That has to be the strangest group of people we've met so far," Tara said, still walking unsteadily from her throbbing and aching pussy.

"Yes," Clover nodded, adjusting her tight bodysuit over her sopping vulva. "And definitely the weirdest sex I've ever had."

"I don't know what you guys are complaining about," Jessop said, his tumescent cock still tingling from the thought of the unusual experiences they'd recently shared. "We got to experience every possible variation of highly erotic sex you could possibly imagine."

"Yeah, and more than one I wouldn't imagine in my wildest *dreams*," Tara chuckled.

Clover peered up into the thick canopy hanging overhead at the abundance of strange wildlife flitting through the trees.

"I have to admit that I'm a little envious of those women with multiple pussies," she nodded. "Can you imagine what it must feel like to orgasm more than once at the same time?"

"*I* certainly can," Jessop said, his organ swelling larger under his tight leggings the more he reflected back on the indigenous people's sexy bodies. "If I had two dicks like those hung tribesmen, I could keep both of you entertained for hours at a time."

"I dunno," Tara grinned. "If we had bodies like the *hermaphrodites*, we could keep *ourselves* entertained as much as we wanted."

"I guess we're just going to have to settle for having sex the same old boring way we're accustomed to," Jessop sighed.

"Don't worry, Jess," Clover said, peering at the growing bulge in his pants. "Something tells me you're going to find plenty of other ways to keep yourself amused from now on."

Jessop noticed a dark animal moving through the thick forest brush and suddenly stopped abruptly.

"I'm feeling the need for a different kind of fulfillment right now," he said, pointing to a large boar clawing for turnips in the fertile soil. "All that crazy sex has built up quite an appetite in my empty stomach."

"Me too," Tara said, motioning for her friends to circle around the animal to block its escape while she slowly pulled an arrow out of the quiver hung over her shoulder.

She placed the arrow on the string of her bow and pulled it back toward her nose while she crept through the underbrush on her tiptoes. When the boar heard the snap of a twig under her foot, he quickly looked up, but it was too late. Tara's practiced aim speared him squarely in the chest, and he fell over onto his side, breathing raggedly. Tara pulled out a knife from her belt and knelt beside the wounded animal, quickly slicing his throat to put it out of his misery.

"You never cease to amaze me," Jessop said, approaching the captured quarry with wide eyes.

"What, with how easily I can capture wild game?" Tara said, looking at him with pinched eyebrows.

"That, and how coldly you can *dispatch* it," he chuckled.

"I say a prayer for every animal before I kill it," Tara huffed. "Every living thing is sacred to me, but at the same time, every form of life is food for someone else, in one form or another."

Clover peered at Jessop disapprovingly, placing her hands on her hips angrily.

"I haven't heard you complaining about Tara's hunting prowess *before*," she said. "You're the one who said you were hungry."

"I'm not complaining," Jessop backpedaled, throwing up his hands defensively. "It's just, you don't expect to see such a cold-blooded killer from such a pretty–"

"*Elf?*" Tara said, staring up at Jessop with a twisted sneer.

"–sexy woman," he said, quickly trying to save face with his newfound friend.

"Well, for that little wisecrack, you can be in charge of cleaning the prey while Clover and I prepare the fire. That is, if you think that's not a womanly enough task for us also..."

"Of course," Jessop smiled. "We're all equals out here in the wilderness. One for all, and all for–"

"*Jessop?*" Clover said, lifting an eyebrow while glaring at her colleague. "Maybe you should have stayed with your new *ladyboy* friend at the camp of mutants. I'm not sure there's enough *cocks* in this triumvirate to satisfy your manly urges."

"Oh, come on," Jessop groaned, crossing his arms over his chest in defeat. "I'm sorry if I offended you. I didn't mean to suggest–"

"It's alright, Jess," Tara said, standing up and handing him her knife as she glanced down at his shriveling organ. "We're just messing with you. Just remember where your meal ticket comes from. You might be handy swinging that big sword of yours in the heat of battle, but we women know how to use our special tools to get what we want also."

"There's no doubt of that," Jessop nodded, grabbing the boar's hind legs and hefting the animal over his back while he headed toward a sturdy tree to hang the beast up in preparation for cleaning. "You guys do your thing while I cut off a drumstick for each of us to eat. It's getting late and we'll need to bed down soon for the night."

Clover paused for a moment while she winked in Tara's direction.

"If you play your cards right and grovel a little more, maybe we'll let you climb into our bedroll tonight to keep you warm," she smiled.

"Oh, I plan on groveling *plenty*," Jessop grinned. "These boar's legs aren't the *only* chunks of juicy meat I plan on feeding you tonight."

2

———

After the three friends filled their stomachs with fresh boar meat, they bedded down together and made love for the rest of the night, falling asleep in each other's arms to affirm their solidarity. After all, they'd been through an unusual variety of escapades in their short time together, both exciting and perilous, and they had no intention of disbanding the unit that had gotten them through the best and worst of times. In the morning, they packed up their belongings and continued through the forest, with no particular destination in mind. Half of the fun of their journey was wandering from one place to another, not knowing what they would encounter next, reveling in the unusual people they met along the way.

After a few hours, they noticed a tall, man-made structure rising above of the treetops a few kilometers away, and they paused to plan their next move.

"What do you think that is?" Clover said, pointing to the unusual structure.

"I'm not sure," Tara said, squinting into the distance with her hand cupped over her eyes to block out the searing overhead sun. "But it's pretty big, so it's probably best we approach it quietly. It looks like a larger civilization than the last one we encountered. We don't know if they'll be hostile or friendly."

"There's no harm in taking a look," Jessop smiled. "If they're anything like the last bunch of woodsmen we met, we could be in for another stimulating surprise."

"*Seriously*, Jess?" Clover said, peering at her friend with an annoyed expression. "Do you *always* think with your dick first? They're just as likely to boil us alive for dinner as jump our bones."

"Clover's right," Tara nodded. "Let's stay together and scope out the place first before we make any introductions. It's better to be safe than end up as human hotdogs."

The trio crept through the brush slowly, keeping their hands close to their weapons in case they encountered any unfriendly natives, but the closer they got to the tall structure, the quieter the forest became.

"There doesn't seem to be any sign of human inhabitation," Clover said, glancing through the thinning clearing at the imposing structure.

"Not on the *ground* at least," Jessop nodded, squinting at the unusual decoration of the palace walls. "But what are those strange figures on the masonry? It almost looks like they're cleaning the surface..."

"That doesn't look like *cleaning* to me," Tara said, creeping closer to the still building. "It looks more like they're–"

"*Fucking!*" Clover said, increasing the speed of her gait as she walked closer to the edifice. "But they're not alive, it seems to be some form of *sculptures*."

"A *lot* of sculptures," Tara nodded. "Hundreds of them."

"And they're all *fornicating*," Jessop said, walking up to

the base of the building and staring at the carnal connec-
tions of the depicted subjects.

"So they are," Tara said. "In every possible combination
and position you could imagine."

"Judging by their strange costumes and jewelry, they
don't look like any people we've seen before," Clover said.

Tara paused for a moment as she scanned the exterior
surface of the building, peering up at the tapering, pyra-
midical shape of the upper ramparts.

"I think it's some kind of *temple*," she nodded. "Possibly
erected by the inhabitants of this area to celebrate their
culture before they moved on or died off. There doesn't
seem to be any sign of life anywhere in the area."

"That's not the *only* thing they erected to celebrate their
culture," Jessop grinned, moving closer to examine one of
the sculptures, twisting his head to decipher how and where
the groups of mostly naked subjects were connecting their
bodies in obvious stages of erotic excitement. "They weren't
shy about placing their organs into whatever moving object
they could find."

"It's fascinating," Clover nodded, walking around the
base of the huge temple and ogling the explicit but beauti-
fully crafted scenes of carnal lovemaking. "They're doing it
in ways I've never seen before."

"And in combinations I never imagined," Tara said,
following closely behind, with her eyes as wide as saucers.

Jessop stopped beside a frieze depicting two women tribbing their pussies together upside down while they stimulated the erect cocks of two men standing beside them,
adjusting his lengthening tool in his pants as he imagined
himself joining in the action.

"This one looks like something *we* should try sometime,"

he chuckled, obviously impressed by the inventive nature of the couplings of the ancient indigenous people.

"That does look pretty hot," Clover said, walking up beside him and staring at the intricate detailing of the women's genitals rubbing together as they bent over each other's bodies.

"Look at their *cocks!*" Tara said, pointing up toward the men's erect organs. "They seem much larger than normal."

"This must have been one hell of a fun place to live back in their day," Jessop nodded, straightening out his hardening tool in his tightening pants. "It's too bad they abandoned this place. We could have kept ourselves amused for *weeks* hooking up with these horny humpers."

"Yes," Clover said, reaching up her hand to caress the pussies of the two women rubbing their vulvas together. "I'd never want to leave a place like this. It seems as close to heaven as you could possibly get."

"Maybe," Tara nodded, sliding her hand up the upturned shaft of one of the men's enormous erections. "There's certainly enough *variety* to keep us distracted for quite some time."

"It's so realistic," Jessop said, stroking his own cock while he watched Tara stimulate the effigied figures. "The carvings are so detailed, it's almost like they're alive."

"I *wish*," Clover said, pressing her middle finger into the cleft of the frieze where the woman on top was rubbing her pussy against the slit of the other woman with her ass raised up in the air.

Suddenly, her eyes bulged open, and she pulled her hand away from the wall, staring at the sculpture in shock.

"Did you *feel* that?" she said, turning toward Tara, who was still stroking her hand up and down the thick shaft of the man standing on the women's right-hand side.

"Feel *what*?" she said. "How lifelike the carvings are? I can almost feel the bulging veins of this guy's hard-on."

"No," Clover said. "Mine *moved*. I swear, it felt like some kind of rumble emanating from the sculpture."

"That's impossible," Tara said, squinting at Clover like she was losing her mind. "These people are made out of stone, they can't move. Maybe you felt some kind of earth tremor or something."

"No," Clover said, returning her hand to the junction of the two women's vulvas and caressing them even harder. "It felt like more of a *throbbing*, like when our pussies contract in the midst of orgasm."

"I think you're letting your fantasies get ahead of reality," Tara chuckled. "There's no way–"

But suddenly, her eyes lit up and she pulled her hand away from the man's bulging cock, staring at the sculpture in shock, just as Clover had.

"See?" Clover said. "Something weird is going on. It's almost like our caresses are bringing these sculptures back to life or something. Maybe the people living here were trapped in the act and pasted on these walls as some form of punishment, like those who allegedly looked at the witch, Medusa."

"Come on, girls," Jessop said, taking a step forward and placing his hand over the erection of the other man standing on the opposite side of the two scissoring women. "I think you're letting your imaginations get ahead of yourselves. Maybe you're hoping *every* man was hung as well as these dudes..."

Suddenly, Jessop's body tensed and his eyes widened while he held his hand still over the base of the second man's dick as he watched some fluid leak out of the tip of its bulbous crown.

"Holy shit!" he exclaimed, hardly believing his eyes.

"I told you," Clover said, beginning to feel her hand lubricating with moisture as the color of the stone images began to slowly soften and darken. "It's almost like they're *enjoying* what we're doing to them. I think they're getting more aroused the more we touch them!"

Tara stepped back toward the amorous foursome and placed both of her hands on the right-hand man's dick, caressing it up and down like she was giving it a handjob, and her eyes bulged as the man's penis began to thicken and throb harder in her hands.

"Oh my God!" she exclaimed, shifting one of her hands over the man's balls and the base of his cock. "You're *right*! I can feel his penis pulsing in my hands. This is crazy!"

As the three friends stroked and rubbed the sculpture subjects' genitals more enthusiastically, suddenly they heard a strange rumbling sound emanating from the surface, while the fornicating group began to moan and move their entire bodies in tandem. Within seconds, their skin turned from the color of white-washed stone to a ruddy pink as they pressed their bodies harder against the determined ministrations of their mesmerized attendants. When the two men's phalluses erupted upwards in long ropes of white semen and the two women's bodies began to shake uncontrollably, jetting equally strong streams of fluid outwards toward the shocked friends like some kind of animated erotic fountain, they peered at one another's dripping faces with shocked but delighted impressions.

Maybe they weren't going to have to settle for plain old boring sex for the rest of their journey, after all.

3

———

After the sexy foursome on the temple wall recovered from their climaxes, they peered down at their liberators with surprised expressions.

"Thank you for freeing us," one of the men said. "Who are you people?"

"We were just about to ask you the same thing," Tara said, wiping the streams of cum off the side of her face. "We're wayward travelers who simply stumbled upon this temple in the wilderness."

"We're Sannyans from the tribe of Santimenis," the woman who had been in the superior position of the tribbing couple replied.

"How did you come to be embalmed in stone on the walls of this temple?" Clover asked.

"Our sheltered tribe had been progressively shrinking from the practice of inbreeding and homo-eroticism," the second man said. "Our king, who had magical powers, decided to turn us into stone as a means of protecting us, hoping that we'd be eventually found and freed by outside visitors."

"Well, it seems that your wishes have come true," Jessop smiled. "What *else* can we do to help your people?"

"You can start by intermingling your seed with our women," the first man said. "The greater our genetic diversity, the greater our chances to survive as a species."

"What about the rest of your trapped friends?" Clover said, glancing up at the multitude of erotic sculptures covering the exterior surface of the temple. "Can't you help free them?"

"I'm afraid only outsiders have been empowered to do so," the man said. "We need sexual engagement with new people to free us from our bonds."

"It will be an arduous task," Jessop nodded, peering up at the stacks of sexy nymphs and buff men adorning the temple. "But if that's the only way, we'll be happy to oblige."

There was an awkward pause, then Clover was the first one to break the silence.

"Where do you want us to get *started*?" she said, just as eager as Jessop to begin uncovering the erotic secrets of this lost civilization.

"You can start with us, if you so desire," the second man said, his thick cock still standing proudly upright and throbbing excitedly over his belly.

"Okay," she said, her eyes darting back and forth between the two men's dripping crowns. "How would you like us to do this, exactly?"

The man glanced at Clover and Tara's lithesome figures, noticing the wet spots in the animal skins covering their private parts.

"We will sit cross-legged on the edge of this tier, while the two women straddle our hips facing one another."

"You mean *Tara* and me?" Clover said, pinching her eyebrows together.

"Yes," the man nodded. "That way, you can enjoy each other's expressions and rub your bodies together while we prod you from behind."

"In our *pussies*?" Clover said, pointing between her legs.

"Yes," the man said.

"Works for me," Clover said as a soft flush rolled over her cheeks while she imagined the pairings in her mind. "What about you, Tara?"

"Absolutely," Tara smiled. "Count me in."

Clover paused as she peered over at the third member of their triumvirate, who was busy staring at the sexy figures of the two women who'd just finished tribbing one another.

"What about *Jessop*?" she said, glancing at her friend. "That leaves two women and only one *cock* in the mix."

The tribeswoman who had previously been on top, peered at the outline of Jessop's upturned erection under his tight pants and smiled.

"He can alternate between probing us one at a time while we assume the yin-yang position."

"The *yin-yang* position?" Jessop said, squinting his eyes in confusion.

"We'll lie down on top of one another and curl our legs upward so you have direct access to each of our yonis," the second woman said. "That way, you can dip your pole in and out of our joined concha, impregnating both of us at the same time when you erupt."

"Huh!" Jessop coughed, barely concealing his excitement at the thought of fucking the two sexy maidens to his heart's desire. "That works for me!"

"Let's assume the positions, then," the first man said, squatting down on the flat surface of the first tier while facing his partner with both of their erections bobbing up against their ripped abs.

The two native women lay down on the warm marble next to them, the first facing upward and the second facing down on top of her, then they curled their knees up tightly against their chests, presenting their dripping pussies joined at their mounds for Jessop's examination. He wasted no time in kneeling behind them, his cock excitedly pointing toward their dripping openings, eager to have his way with the prostrated nymphs. At the same time, Clover and Tara squatted over the laps of the two men, facing one another as their eyes bulged open in excitement at the prospect of impaling themselves on their giant, pulsing organs. They angled their hips backward, pointing the native men's crowns toward their dripping slits then slowly lowered themselves over their thick shafts until they were stretched to their limits.

"Oh my God," Clover huffed, staring at Tara kneeling directly in front of her. "Do you feel what I feel?"

"If you mean the biggest cock I've had inside my pussy since our encounter with those oversize *dwarfs*, yes," Tara grunted. "You weren't kidding about this place being heaven on earth."

"Fuck, yes," Clover groaned, flexing her thighs as she slowly pumped her body up and down over the hung tribesman's throbbing pole. "I can see where their magical powers come from. This guy's dick is stretching me so wide, I can feel my clit rubbing against his shaft."

Tara glanced down, peering at Clover's hard nub disappearing in and out of her folds as she fucked the man's giant organ, then she leaned forward to kiss her on the lips, rubbing their breasts together while they humped their partners in unison.

"*Ungh*," Clover moaned into Tara's mouth as they rocked their bodies together. "If this is what heaven looks like, sign me up. I can see now why these people never wanted to travel beyond their sheltered community. They seem to have taken the art of lovemaking to an entirely new plane."

"Yes," Tara groaned, twirling her tongue inside Clover's mouth while she humped her partner's organ more aggressively. "I hardly even want to *come*. I could do this all day."

Clover heard some loud grunting sounds emanating from the figures beside her and she peered over at Jessop, who had a look of utter rapture on his face as he humped the backsides of the two women joined together in a cocoon position.

"I'm not sure we can say the same thing about Jessop," she giggled. "I don't think he's had this much fun since he had sex with that hung hermaphrodite in the tribe of mutants. It looks like he's about to have a stroke over there while he's fucking the two women's joined pussies."

"Good for him," Tara chuckled, glancing in his direction. "He could use a little distraction to keep him busy for a while. Sex is the only thing he's had on his mind these past few days."

Clover peered up at the plethora of erotic sculptures adorning the other layers of the pyramid and smiled.

"Well, judging by the availability of willing partners for his amusement, I'm sure he'll expend most of his energies pretty soon, discovering all the novel ways he can have sex. These people give new meaning to the expression working outside the box."

"All the more for *us*, then," Tara groaned, feeling the pleasure spreading in her midsection. "We'd better finish up here soon so we've got enough time to free the rest of the trapped natives."

"I couldn't hold it much longer if I tried," Clover said,

thrusting her tongue deeper inside Tara's mouth. "I'm about to have the biggest orgasm I've had in a long time."

"Me too," Tara huffed. "Hold me while I squirt all over your pussy. Let's see if we can get these guys to spill their seeds a little more quickly."

While Tara and Clover pressed their hips down into their partners' laps, the men circled their legs around each of the women's hips, pulling their bodies closer together.

"Oh *fuck*," Clover panted into Tara's mouth while a deep flush spread over her bouncing breasts. "I'm going to come so hard..."

When they heard Jessop groaning in delirious pleasure as he curled his torso over the two tribeswomen's bodies in simultaneous pleasure, they grunted loudly as they squirted their combined juices over the tribesmen's grinding balls, feeling their cocks jetting their semen against the far reaches of their convulsing pussies. It seemed to take almost as long for everybody to enjoy the final throes of their climaxes as it had for them to build up to this point, and while the group grunted and moaned in exalted harmony, they savored every second of their newfound unions. When they finally stopped shaking and convulsing, they held each other for a long still moment, as if to allow their partners' seeds time to spread upward to find fertile new ground.

4

———

When the group finally separated their bodies and lay down beside one another, completely spent, Clover peered up at the two men, caressing their throbbing cocks as the last of their semen spilled out onto the ledge of the temple wall.

"Thanks for that," she said. "That was the most enlightened sex I've had in a long time. What will you do now?"

"We'll have to leave our homeland," one of the men said. "The only way for our people to survive now is to spread our seeds as far and wide as we can to preserve our genetic heritage."

"What about us?" Tara said. "We could assist in that endeavor if we were to stay with your people for a while..."

"There's only three of you, and *hundreds* of us," the second man said. "With the long gestation period to produce new offspring, it would take many generations to erase the damage of successive inbreeding. I'm afraid the only way to ensure our survival is to mix with as many new partners as we can."

"Lucky for *them*," Clover sighed. "We'll do our best to free the rest of your tribe as quickly as we can, but it may take some time."

"My people aren't going anywhere in the meantime," the man said, peering upward at the stacks of embalmed tribespeople. "I'm sure they'll be happy to experience your special attention and their newfound freedom."

"Good luck then on your continued journey," Tara said. "Thank you for sharing your gifts with us."

"Namaste, my friends," the other man said, cupping his hands together and bowing gracefully before standing up and holding out his hands to help the other women up from their prone positions.

While Clover, Tara, and Jessop watched the foursome disappear quietly into the woods, they peered at one another with wide smiles.

"Was that as much fun for you as it was for us, Jessop?" Clover said, staring down at her friend's throbbing organ.

"It was *incredible*," Jessop nodded. "I haven't come that long and hard for as long as I can remember."

"I'm glad," Clover said. "Were you able to share some of that pleasure *equally* between the two women?"

"I'm not sure about equally," Jessop chuckled. "But I tried my best to inject my semen in each of their pulsing pussies while I enjoyed the longest orgasm of my life."

Clover nodded while she peered upward at the tiered layers of erotic sculptures stacked above them in the giant temple.

"Do you think you've got any juice left in the tank?" she said. "Because if we tackle only one of these every day, it'll take us *months* to free the rest of the entombed tribespeople."

"I think I've got a couple more sessions left in me for

today at least," Jessop nodded as his penis began to swell while he scanned the scenes of the other exotic couplings.

The women paused as they peered around them at the various forms of the frozen figures.

"Why don't we try to find a group with two men and one woman next?" Tara said. "That way, our pairings will be a little more balanced, and we can give each of our partners our full attention."

"Sounds good to me," Clover nodded. "Will that work for you, Jessop?"

"I suppose so," Jessop frowned. "Although the more, the merrier. After all, I've only got one dick, and there's at least a *hundred* pussies to inseminate in this temple."

"Let's see what we can find then," Tara said, glancing around her to find the next suitable match-up. "We can start at the bottom and work our way up, to make sure we don't miss anyone."

The trio climbed down from the ledge and slowly walked around the perimeter of the palace while they ogled the various couplings of the naked subjects.

"What about this one?" Clover said, stopping beside a frieze depicting a man humping a bent-over woman while she fellated the cock of a second man kneeling in front of her.

"Been there, done that," Jessop huffed, looking for something more interesting to excite his flagging tool.

"How about *this* one, then?" Tara said, pointing to a teetering trio of figures positioned in a pyramid position, with each person's face buried between one of the other's legs.

"Too acrobatic," Jessop said, furrowing his brow. "I'd be afraid of falling over the whole time I'm going down on my partner."

"Okay," Clover said, pausing to inspect yet another novel hookup pattern.

This one showed a woman lying face-up on the ground while one man knelt over her face as he bent over, with another man fucking her pussy as he leaned forward, licking the first man's upturned ass.

"*That* looks interesting," Jessop nodded, his dick flexing unconsciously as he imagined being stimulated from two sides at the same time. "But there'll be *six* of us in the mix, with only two people lying down."

"I'm sure we can find a way for Tara and me to keep one of the men amused while you throat-fuck the third woman," Clover smiled. "That is, if you don't mind having your ass licked by another man..."

"Something tells me I won't be thinking about the sex of the person behind me while I'm getting sucked off by the woman on the floor," Jessop chuckled. "Especially if I'm watching you two getting fucked by the third man."

"Let's do it then," Tara said, climbing up onto the ledge to caress the balls of the man kneeling over the prone woman's crotch.

5

———————

Clover and Jessop followed Tara's lead, alternately stimulating the woman's stone breasts and the man's thick tool impaled in her mouth. Within seconds, a familiar rumble could be heard, and the embalmed trio's skin soon turned soft and flush as their figures began to move while they panted and moaned in unison. It didn't take long for their bodies to begin shaking and quivering while they enjoyed a simultaneous climax.

"Hello," Clover smiled when the trio stopped quivering. "We're from a place far away. How would you like to try doing that with some *different* partners?"

"Our master told us this would happen someday," the man who had been on the back end of the trio said. "Are you familiar with our customs?"

"If you mean the different techniques your people use to join together in carnal union, we're just starting to figure that out. The carvings of your erotic temple have really opened our eyes to the unique ways men and women can enjoy each other's bodies."

"What would you like to try?" the man who was being

fellated said, darting his eyes between the newcomer's naked bodies.

Clover paused for a moment while she smiled at Tara and Jessop.

"I think our friend Jessop here had in mind taking over your position, if the lady is willing to suck another cock..."

The newly awakened native woman glanced at Jessop's rising pole and licked her lips.

"It's a little smaller than I'm accustomed to," she chuckled. "So I shouldn't have much trouble taking it all the way down my throat. But what will the rest of you do?"

Now it was Tara's turn to provide more detail for their lascivious plan.

"Perhaps the man who was in front previously would like to try fucking you from the *other* end this time while we keep your other partner stimulated in another way? Something tells me he'll be more than enough man for both of us."

"That should be fun to watch," the woman nodded. "I've never seen the way outsiders have sex before. Plus, having *two* women to inject his seed into will assist the development of our race."

"Yes," Clover grinned. "Especially since our friend will be wasting his seed by injecting it down your *throat*."

"I'm sure we can fix that soon enough," the nymph smiled at Jessop.

"Shall we get started then?" Tara said, noticing the sun beginning to cast a shadow over the side of the temple. "We don't have much time left in the day to free the rest of your compatriots."

"Feel free," the woman said, reclining onto her back and spreading her knees apart as the man behind her stood up and the second man moved between her legs.

While Jessop kneeled in front of the girl, angling his now fully erect penis toward her glistening lips, the third man joined Clover and Tara as they pressed him down toward the sun-dappled marble. He sat with his legs extended straight and his big pole standing up in his lap, then Clover and Tara squatted down over his hips facing one another, pressing their sopping pussies together against the base of his dick while they stroked the rest of his long shaft with two hands.

"Uhhhn," the native man groaned, enjoying the ministrations of the sexy newcomers.

"Do you *like* that?" Clover smiled, flapping her thumb over his dripping glans while he flexed his buttock muscles, trying to thrust his organ up between their bellies. "Is this something you've tried before?"

"It's certainly different with *outsiders*," he grunted, pinching their pink nipples as the two women polished his upturned phallus like a brass bed pole.

By now, Jessop had inserted the entire length of his throbbing organ into the pretty native woman's mouth, hunched over her head while he plowed his dick as deep into her cavity as he could. She had no difficulty taking his entire length while she relaxed her throat muscles, humming contentedly as her body bounced back and forth from the action of the second man pounding her from the other end. Jessop seemed to be pacing himself as he enjoyed the feeling of being deep-throated by his willing partner, but when the man behind him leaned forward and began to lick his sphincter, he threw his head back, moaning in intense pleasure.

"That seems to be something Jessop's never experienced before," Tara chuckled, watching him hump the woman's face harder and more excitedly.

"Which *part*?" Clover smiled, turning to watch the other trio. "Getting his cock deep-throated, or having his butthole licked at the same time?"

"Both," Tara laughed. "I'm not sure it bothers him in the slightest that it's a *guy* licking his ass from behind."

"How quickly the tables are turned," Clover smiled. "I have a feeling more than his eyes will be opened by these erotic tribespeople before we're done with them."

"Speaking of which," Tara said, noticing the man's cock sliding up between their bellies was emitting progressively more seminal fluid. "Maybe we should give this guy something *tighter* to rub his cock against. It would be a shame to waste any more of his seed."

"You're reading my mind," Clover nodded. "Which of us will go first?"

"I don't think it matters, since he's probably got more than enough for both of us. Why don't you take the first turn and when he starts spurting, let me take over?"

"You're twisting my arm, girl," Clover smiled, rising up on her knees and pointing the tip of the man's organ into her opening and sitting down over his shaft until it was embedded all the way up into her pulsating pussy.

"I'll never get tired of this feeling," Clover huffed while her pupils dilated as she stared at Tara with unbridled lust.

"I don't imagine," Tara chuckled, pinching Clover's nipples to bring her closer to her peak.

At the same time, she reached down between the man's legs and squeezed his balls tighter as they began to curl up toward Clover's dripping pussy.

"I think he's getting close," Tara said, watching the color of his erection growing darker. "Get ready to jump off after you come..."

"You won't have to wait very long," Clover huffed,

bouncing faster over the native man's huge cock. "I'm almost there."

Suddenly, she raised her pussy over the top of the man's pulsing organ, spraying her juices over Tara's and the native man's lower extremities, then Tara jumped just as quickly atop his spurting instrument, groaning loudly as she flapped her thighs against the sides of his tightening stomach.

"Holy shit!" Tara squealed. "Just when I thought this couldn't get better. I think this guy is squirting even harder inside me than the last one. I hope you're ready to have *babies* sometime soon!"

"Maybe," Clover smiled as she squeezed her friend's tits while Tara gushed over her partner's pulsating organ. "We can't keep wandering aimlessly through these woods forever. I suppose we should settle down and raise a family eventually. This place seems as good as any."

Tara nodded while she glanced over at Jessop, who was wailing at the top of his lungs as he emptied his seed deep inside the native girl's gullet while the man behind him tickled his anus with his tongue

"We'll have to share the spoils with Jessop," she said. "He might want a few of his own kids running around the neighborhood. It seems all of his *other* partners will soon be abandoning him for greener pastures."

"No worries," Clover nodded. "We'll make sure he has a few other fertile valleys to sow his oats. We're going to be all he's got after these tribespeople drift away."

"Well, at least he'll have a lot of new *positions* to try out to keep us stimulated for a while," Tara chuckled. "I haven't seen him this excited since we discovered that island of Amazon women."

"I have a feeling he'll have broadened his sexual preferences a little by the time we're finished here."

"Yeah, we might have to look for a few more *male-male* pairings with our next tryst," Tara said.

"As long as he can keep it *up*," Clover nodded, glancing up at the tall column of erotic friezes. "Something tells me these statues have a lot more repressed sexual energy than we do."

6

———

fter their new partners recovered from their erotic awakening and shortly after left the temple, the three friends decided to rest to recharge their sexual energy. Jessop in particular seemed especially depleted, with his limp cock hanging like a soggy noodle after coming so hard from his last pairing.

"What do you think, Jessop?" Tara teased. "Did you enjoy that last hookup? You seemed to enjoy being stimulated from behind by that hunky native man. Maybe you'd like a little more *anal* action in our next go-round?"

"I'm not sure I can take much more of this," Jessop chuckled. "That's two insane orgasms I've just had. I don't think I've got much more juice to share, if that's our primary objective here."

Clover glanced up, noticing another sculpture two levels above them where the natives were stacked together in an act of auto-fellatio.

"Maybe we won't *have* to this time," she said. She pointed to the group of subjects with their legs swung over their heads as they stimulated their own genitals. "How would you like to learn how to suck your own cock?"

Jessop twisted his head and when he saw the group of natives with their stone dicks embedded in their own mouths, his cock stirred immediately.

"Now *that* would be a useful skill to learn for quiet days when there's no one around," he smiled. "Especially when you two are self-absorbed pleasing one another."

"Speaking of which," Tara said, peering at the exotic scene. "Isn't that a *girl* sandwiched in the middle of the group? How on earth is she managing to lick her own pussy?"

"I don't know," Clover said. "But I'd sure like to find out. Let's check it out."

The trio climbed up the two levels, then they stared at the sculpture, tilting their heads from side to side trying to ascertain how the embedded figures had managed to bend their bodies far enough to lick their own genitals.

"Okay," Clover said after a moment. "The trick seems to be to lie on your back and use the weight of your lower body raised over your head to push your crotch toward your face..."

"I must have tried that a million times," Jessop chuckled. "I could never seem to get closer than a few inches from the tip of my tool, even with my tongue stretched out as far as it will go."

"Yeah, well your dick's not as long as these guys," Clover kidded.

"But the girl in the middle is licking her *pussy*," Tara said. "I think there's more to it than that."

Clover took a longer moment to study the frieze, stepping closer as she placed her hand atop the backs of the stacked figures.

"They're resting their bodies on top of one another," she nodded. "Maybe the additional weight of the figures above them is enough to bend their bodies that little extra needed distance."

"There's only one way to find out," Tara said, reaching forward to caress the cock of the male figure on the bottom of the stack to bring him to life. "We'll have to revive them from their slumber and ask them first-hand."

Following Tara's lead, Clover and Jessop stepped closer to stroke the other two figures in the carving. Sure enough, as with the other sculptures, the figures soon began to move as their skin slowly turned pink and the three individuals depicted in the scene began to moan and shake. The three friends watched in fascination while each of the newly freed Sannyans squirted in their own mouths as their buttocks quivered in pleasure.

"Holy fuck!" Clover said, watching the girl in the middle of the stack sucking her clit as her legs trembled above her head.

"I'm *definitely* game for this one," Jessop nodded, his dick rapidly rising above his belly with newfound energy.

After they finished climaxing, the three natives slowly separated themselves, then they stood up, peering at their liberators.

"Thank you," the woman who'd been in the middle said. "We've waited far too long to finish this."

"I'll bet," Tara chuckled. "Can you teach us how to do that?"

"I suppose so," the native girl said. "It's mostly a matter of relaxing your body and *meditating* than anything else. The more you relax your muscles, the more easily you'll be able to curl your body and bend your spine."

Clover peered over at the two men, whose dicks were dripping long strings of cum onto the hot marble ledge.

"You seemed to be getting a little help from your *friends*," she said. "Is it necessary to stack your bodies in such a manner to reach your own organs?"

"It helps a little," the girl nodded. "But we do that more as a means of sharing our chakra than forcing our bodies into position. You newcomers might find it a little difficult to balance your bodies that way the first time."

"Can you help us some other way then?" Jessop said. "We never been able to accomplish this, no matter how hard we've tried."

"I think so," the woman smiled. "If you lie down in the forward-fold position as we did, each of us can assist you to achieve the necessary degree of extension."

"Okay," Clover said, lying down on the marble and flipping her legs over her chest until her toes lay on the floor above her head. "You mean like this?"

"Yes," the woman said, kneeling behind Clover's upturned ass and resting her bare chest over Clover's glistening pussy, slowly pushing her further forward.

Tara and Jessop mimicked Clover's pose, and the two native men who had been stacked together with the native girl took up similar positions behind their buttocks.

"Now, try to relax your muscles and not focus on the destination so much," the native girl said in a soothing voice. "The key is to let all the other distractions of the moment slip away while you become one with your bodies."

The three friends could feel their bodies contracting a few more inches while their partners gently pressed their torsos against their arching backs.

"Yes," the native girl purred. "That's the idea. Close your eyes and let your body fully relax. Feel your toes moving behind your head like you're walking on sand. It should be a relaxing feeling, not one of pressure and strain."

"I can feel it," Jessop said, opening one eye and noticing his bobbing cock inching closer to his mouth. The fact that another buff native man was pressing his muscular chest against his ass with his breath fluttering down over his stretching anus only served to make him even harder.

"Don't open your eyes yet," the native girl admonished, glancing over in Jessop's direction. "It will only stop you from reaching your objective. Instead, focus on the sensation of your lingam entering your cavity and savor the feeling of your soft tongue on your sensitive tissues..."

"Mmmf!" Jessop groaned when he felt his swelling crown slide over his lips. He couldn't believe the sensation of sucking his own cock, and it was difficult to resist the impulse of rocking his hips to create more friction.

"Try to avoid jerking your body," the girl said. "This will only impede the relaxation of your muscles. The key is to push slowly forward, then rest for a moment while you relax your muscles as you feel the tension disappearing from your body. Allow your tongue to stimulate your sex organ, not the movement of your hips."

Jessop concentrated on following the girl's instruction, and before long, he could slowly feel his pole pushing deeper into his mouth. At the same time, his partner blew his breath softly over his exposed ass and flexing anus, creating a sensation he'd never experienced before.

Meanwhile, Clover and Tara, who had been following the girl's instructions more patiently, had bent their bodies into an even more compressed position as their hips continued moving closer to their faces. Clover could feel the scent of her pussy nearing her nose, and when she felt a drop of lubrication falling on her face, she grunted in excitement. She wanted to look up at the pretty native girl hunched over her as she slowly pressed her body forward, but she knew that would just cause her to lose focus and tense up further. For now at least, she'd have to be content imagining the sight of the girl's eyes watching her labia spread apart and her tingling bulb growing harder as it began to poke out of its protective hood.

Tara was similarly distracted, knowing the native man who'd partnered with her had his face only inches away from her own throbbing pussy, and part of her wished he'd bury his face in her moist cleft and suck her clit even before she might have a chance to do so. But as she arched her back further downward toward her face with the help of his gentle prodding, she could feel the heat of her sex close to her lips and she unconsciously opened her mouth, awaiting the magic prize. When the two women felt their dripping vulvas finally touch their lips, they groaned softly, eagerly extending their tongues to bathe their burning bulbs with their soft tongues. The feeling of licking their own pussies was completely different from licking another woman's vulva, and they reveled in the sensation as they teased and probed their swelling slits.

Sandwiched between the two others, Jessop felt his own organ pressing deeper into his cavity as his muscular partner continued pressing steadily on his backside, until Jessop gagged when he felt his glans press against the back of his throat. His partner released the pressure momentarily, to let Jessop adjust to the unique feeling of swallowing his own cock.

"Relax your jaw when you feel your sex reaching the limits of its movement," the girl instructed all three of the excited participants. "Explore all of the regions of your perineum with your eyes and your fingers, and savor the taste of your beautiful organs. For the young man, if you relax your throat and concentrate on breathing through your nose, you'll find you can press your instrument even deeper."

Jessop paused as he focused on breathing through his nose, then he nodded to his partner to resume his pressure as his cock began to stretch the back of his throat and his shaft started to slide down the opening to his gullet. The sensation of feeling his own erect penis slipping down his throat was utterly sublime, and he stretched his lips wider until he felt his balls resting against his chin. Unsure what to do next, he opened his eyes and the man behind him nodded, slowly lowering his head onto his exposed anus, circling his tongue over his sphincter as it spasmed in excitement. Jessop grunted loudly, discovering it felt even better when he was sucking his own cock, and he curled his knees behind his head to lock his body into position so he could focus on the exquisite feeling of the other man licking his sensitive butthole while his throbbing erection pulsed in this throat.

As he was enjoying the most transcendent erotic experience of his life, his two friends were moaning equally loud beside him while they lapped up the juices rolling down the front of their slits, sucking their burning jewels into their mouths and rolling their tongues over their tingling buttons with unbridled glee while their partners looked on. But it wasn't until the second man and the pretty native girl lowered their heads onto their pulsing rosebuds that the two prostrated friends began to grunt and wail in tandem. With all three of the friends now squirming and shaking uncontrollably, it was no longer possible to maintain any pretense of relaxation, as their impending orgasms built to an undeniable crescendo as they locked their faces onto their quivering groins in sheer rapture.

When they finally erupted in ecstatic unison, Jessop choked momentarily while his organ pulsed in his mouth and he felt every squirt of his ejaculate sliding down his willing throat. To assist with the emptying of his seed, the native man who was licking his pucker reached up and squeezed his balls, only adding to the incredible sensation of having his entire erogenous zone stimulated simultaneously. Meanwhile, Clover and Tara's partners inserted three fingers into their pulsating pussies while they trilled their spasming sphincters with their tongues as the women's clits twitched in their own mouths. The force of their fingers in the women's holes caused their pent-up juices to fly even further and farther outward, bathing each of their faces and even Jessop's convulsing body lying next to them. By the time the trio finished shaking and gushing, they collapsed onto the puddle of liquid forming on the warm marble floor, watching the setting sun streaming through the surrounding trees, bathing them in light like a divine force was peering down on them.

It was a perfect way to end their first day exploring the exotic temple, and the three of them soon fell asleep lying next to one another, dreaming of more exciting combinations to come.

7

When the three friends woke up the following morning, they slowly flitted their eyes open, listening to the sound of the birds singing in the surrounding forest. Their stomachs were grumbling from not having eaten for almost twenty-four hours while they distracted themselves at the sexual banquet of the erotic temple. They climbed down from their perch and caught some wild rabbits, then had a picnic at the base of the temple while roasting the game on a spit over a fire.

"Well," Clover said, glancing up at the tall tower. "At least we managed to free a *dozen* or so imprisoned natives yesterday."

"Yes," Tara nodded, peering around the base of the temple while counting the number of friezes remaining on each side. "But there's roughly ten sculptures on each side of the pyramid, so it'll take us at least two weeks before we liberate the rest of the people just on the bottom tier."

"True," Jessop said, darting his eyes upward toward the top of the structure. "But each tier is smaller than the one below, so the number of pairings grows smaller the higher up we go."

"Unless there's even *more* frozen people inside the temple," Clover mused.

"I didn't see an entrance anywhere on the outside," Tara said. "Maybe it's sealed, like some kind of giant tomb..."

"Or maybe there's a secret entrance that will only be revealed when we free all the people on the outside," Jessop suggested.

"I guess there's only one way to find out," Clover nodded, standing up and wiping her face with the back of her hand as she finished picking the meat off the last rabbit carcass. "We better get back at it if we're only going to manage a few pairings every day. I'm not sure my aching pussy can take more than a couple of these Sannyans' big dicks at a time. We're going to have to pace ourselves if we're going to finish this job anytime soon."

"Maybe we can find a scene depicting only *women* this time?" Tara nodded, rubbing her swollen pussy softly with her hand.

"That works for *me*," Jessop grinned, his tool starting to harden as he imagined the cornucopia of erotic delights awaiting him on the gleaming tower.

The trio began to walk around the base of the tower, searching for an entrance to the structure while simultaneously appraising the formations of the frozen figures. When they reached halfway around the structure, Clover stopped in front of a frieze showing three women in a tangled union.

"Look at *this* one," she said to the others. "There's no men involved this time, and it seems to be another position we've never tried."

"Yes," Tara nodded, squinting at the joined threesome. "But how are they stimulating each of their *pussies* in that position? I don't see any direct contact between their genitals."

Jessop stepped closer to the wall, rubbing his hand softly over one of the women's hips.

"Two of them seem to be wearing some kind of a *belt* over their hips," he said. "Maybe they're using some kind of–"

"Dildos!" Clover said, widening her eyes.

"Now *that* sounds like an intriguing hookup," Tara nodded excitedly.

"Yes," Clover said, pressing her face up toward the surface of the sculpture and examining the shape of the improvised phalluses the women were using. "And they're considerably smaller than the size of the other men's dicks, so it will be a little easier for us to accommodate their couplings..."

"What about *me* though?" Jessop said, pinching his eyebrows together. "How am *I* going to get in on the action with two women wearing strap-on cocks?"

"That's a good point," Clover said, stepping back to consider the possibilities.

Then her lips slowly curled upward as she began to formulate a plan.

"What if you knelt behind the girl on top and fucked her from behind while I take the position of the girl underneath while she fucks me with the dildo?"

"Then what about the other two women?" Tara said, peering at the figure on the bottom who was penetrating the girl wedged in the middle with a second dildo while lying prostrated on the ground.

"You could take the position of the middle girl, while she moves between your legs to lick your two pussies," Clover nodded.

"That sounds perfect," Tara grinned, imagining the sexy configuration. "You're a genius!"

"Shall we get started awakening these sexy maidens then?" Clover grinned.

"Damn right," Jessop nodded, curling his hand under the ass of the woman on top to caress her exposed slit.

Clover slipped her hand between the parted legs of the middle woman, then Tara started to caress the breasts of the woman on the bottom, watching the color of the stone slowly beginning to lighten as the joined figures began to rumble and moan. When their skin transformed fully to flesh and their bodies were able to move freely, the threesome began to shake their bodies together, fucking each other vigorously at the hips. Clover, Tara, and Jessop watched with increasing arousal as they stimulated the women more rapidly while the women on the temple wall stretched their mouths open, moaning in escalating pleasure until all three of them quivered together in climactic union.

8
____

"Hello," Tara smiled, while she peered at the bodies of the dripping women as they collapsed onto the warm marble surface of the temple floor. "We're here to free you from your bonds."

"Thank you," one of the women said. "What can we do to repay the gift you've given us?"

"Well," Tara smiled. "We'd love to join you in your little party if you're willing to welcome a few extra participants..."

"We're always happy to welcome outsiders to our sexual activities," the second woman nodded, staring at Jessop's stiffening tool. "Especially if it involves another man who's willing to share his seed."

"My seed is always willing," Jessop chuckled, his cock bobbing excitedly above his navel.

"How exactly would you like to do this?" the third woman said. "Since we've got _three_ phalluses and three yonis?"

Clover paused as she stared at the pretty native women's figures.

"Perhaps the two who were on the top and bottom would

like some more *direct* stimulation this time?" she said. "I'm thinking of two different pairings–"

"I like the sound of that," the girl who'd been on the bottom said, spreading her knees further apart, inviting the newcomers to join her. "But which of us will get to enjoy the *boy's* dripping tool?"

"I was thinking you could fuck me with your pretty pole," Tara said, staring at the carved wooden peg strapped around her waist. "While the one in the middle kneels behind us, stimulating us with her tongue..."

"That sounds even better," the girl on the bottom smiled, signaling for the second girl to move into position as Tara knelt between her legs facing away, presenting her dripping pussy for her wide eyes.

"And what would you like *me* to do?" the woman had been on the top of the tribbing trio said, peering at Clover's pale figure and Jessop's bright pink erection.

"I'd like you to fuck me with that hard dick of yours," Clover said, kneeling beside the other threesome and tilting her glistening pussy upwards for the examination of the third girl. "While my friend Jessop fucks you equally hard from behind."

"Okay," the third girl nodded. "As long as he pokes his pole in my *concha* instead of my pucker. We need to spread your seeds as much as possible for our people to thrive and propagate."

"So we've heard," Jessop grinned. "We're happy to oblige, believe me."

"Alright then," the girl nodded, positioning the tip of her dildo in front of Clover's dripping slit as Jessop moved behind her. When he rammed his dick into her pussy, she lurched forward, slamming her own pole deep into Clover's waiting cavity.

Within seconds, all six partners were rocking their bodies together, moaning and watching each other enjoy another novel connection of mingling body parts and moving figures.

"Is it just *me*?" Clover squinted while she peered over at Tara, who was humping her partner's phallus just as hard as she was. "Or is your dildo starting to feel *warm and fleshy* like a man's dick?"

"Yes," Tara grunted, arching her back as the second girl knelt between her legs and flapped her nub with the tip of her tongue. "I think these Sannyans have some *other* magical powers they haven't been telling us about."

"Well, they *did* say they needed to spread their seeds as wide as possible," Clover grinned, pressing her hips backwards against the third woman's humping hips.

"This whole experience is growing weirder by the moment," Tara nodded, throwing her head back as a deep flush began to spread over her bouncing tits.

"What about you, Jessop?" Clover said, twisting her head behind her to peer at her friend who was grabbing hold of the girl kneeled between her legs while humping her ass. "Are you finding this experience just as magical as we are?"

"Fuck, yes," he hissed, staring at the girl lying next to them while she flexed her meaty pole deeper into Tara's tunnel. "I can't wait to switch positions with you guys when we're finished so I can play with those sexy girls' dicks when they're finished with you..."

"You might have to wait for the next pairing," Tara said, arching her back as she felt the pleasure spreading over her body. "But something tells me you won't have much trouble finding more of these multi-talented natives on the rest of the temple. I have a feeling there's plenty more of this where it came from."

"This is too hot," Jessop nodded as his arm muscles began to tense while he gripped the ass of the woman in front of him. "I'm going to come soon. I can't hold it much longer."

"Don't waste your energy," Clover said, angling her head down and peering between her legs at his tightening balls while he slammed them against the native girl's dripping pussy. "Plant your seed as soon as you can so we can move on to the rest of the tribe. I'm almost ready to shoot off also. What about you Tara?"

"Are you *kidding* me?" Tara panted. "I've just been waiting for the rest of you. Let's show these girls how hard we can squirt with the rest of them. Are you ready for some fireworks?"

"Let it go, baby," Clover growled, humping her hips harder against the native girl's throbbing organ. "Let me watch you spray your juices all over the girl's face planted between your legs."

"God, yes," Tara squealed. "I'm going to come so hard–"

Suddenly, she lifted her hips higher in the air while the girl underneath kept her dick glued to her pussy as the other girl mashed her face between Tara's widening legs, then her juices started spraying out in every direction as her hips shook and trembled in intense pleasure. When Clover saw her friend climaxing on top of the native girl's pulsing organ, she lost all remaining control, releasing the built-up pressure that had been building in her hips, squirting all over Jessop's balls and the third girl's throbbing vulva.

When Jessop felt his friend gushing over his tightening balls, he hunched over the native girl's back, squeezing her tits hard while she trembled and quivered along with the others. As with their previous pairings, it seemed to take forever for everyone to stop pulsing and shaking in ecstatic climax before the six of them collapsed onto the warm marble surface, peering up at the frozen images of the other natives who seemed to be staring back at them in simultaneous pleasure.

"Holy shit," Jessop panted in exhausted contentment. "This only seems to get better with every episode. How many different ways have these people figured out to have sex with one another?"

"I don't know," Tara said, staring up at the stacks of fornicating figures entombed above them. "But now that we know these women can transform into men, something tells me we're not going to get tired of finding out."

Clover paused as she peered up at a sculpture showing three men sitting in a circle while they rubbed their dicks together in a tantric trance.

"Maybe the same thing is true of the *men*," she said, her mind beginning to race ahead with visions of other exciting hookups.

"If only some of that magic could rub off on *us*," Tara nodded. "I wouldn't mind having a dick of my own for a day or two while I sampled a few more of these sexy nymphs plastered on the wall."

"You're reading my mind, girl," Clover smiled, peering over at Jessop's throbbing tool, dripping its cum onto the marble surface of the temple floor. "If they're looking to spread more of their seed with outside visitors, Jessop's not the *only* one who's willing to share his juice with the rest of the clan..."

9

———

The three friends climbed up to the next level to peer at the entombed men rubbing their dicks together in a circle, pinching their eyebrows together trying to figure out how they were going to configure the new pairing.

"How's this going to work?" Jessop said, shaking his head. "Now there's four cocks, and only two women."

Clover, who always seemed to be two steps ahead of her friends dreaming up new sexual combinations, paused for a moment as she considered the possibilities.

"Well," she nodded after a few moments. "Since the theme of this scene seems to be rubbing genitals together, there are a number of ways we can do this. What if one of the three men breaks away while Tara and I trib our pussies against his tool, while you do the same with the other two?"

"My dick will get absolutely *swallowed up* by those guys' hard-ons," Jessop said, beginning to feel envious of their oversize erections.

"Come on, Jess," Tara chuckled, noticing his cock starting to bob upward as he stared at their huge organs. "We know you like playing with *guys* almost as much as women. Their dicks will be hardly a match for your own impressive instrument."

"We might be able to make it work," Jessop nodded, imagining his prick rubbing up against the other mens' sexy organs.

"Alright then," Clover smiled. "Shall we get started awakening them?"

"Fuck, yes," Tara grinned. "I can't wait to see these guys shoot off together!"

They stepped forward and began to stimulate the trapped native's upturned organs, and within seconds, their throbbing tools began to turn fleshy and pink as they humped their bodies together.

"Fuck, that's *hot*," Clover said, stroking one of the men's erections harder as his pre-cum began to spill over his crown and drip down over the sides of their joined tools.

"I could do this all day," Tara nodded, interlacing her fingers with her friends as she squeezed the native men's tools tighter together.

"I wish I had a cock this big," Jessop frowned. "I'd have no shortage of willing partners wherever we traveled."

"Don't sell yourself short, Jess," Tara said, peering at his bouncing hard-on. "You're hung better than most men. Plus, you're a lot more *handsome* than these oversize brutes."

"And you've got two willing girls to play with everywhere we go," Clover smiled. "This is just a temporary side distraction."

"I think it's a little more than a *distraction*," Jessop panted, stroking the native men's intertwined cocks together with increasing arousal. "It's more like a *feast for the senses*."

Clover paused for a moment, noticing the cheeks of the

three native men growing ruddier as their crowns began to swell even larger.

"You better watch out," she said. "I think these guys are about to erupt any moment now. Maybe we should stand back and let them finish off by themselves so we're not completely covered in cum."

"Yeah," Tara said, loosening her grip on the three men's dripping organs. "Let's save that for the *next* round."

The three friends stepped away from the frotting group, then the native men pressed their heads closer together, thrusting their tongues in each other's mouths while they rubbed their cocks with their joined hands. As their organs seemed to grow purpler by the moment, they grunted loudly in each other mouths, until they suddenly arched their backs together, erupting in a fountain of cum spraying high over their heads. Clover, Tara, and Jessop watched in amazement at the muscular trio while they sprayed their juices up in the air like some kind of erotic Greek statue.

When the men finally finished shaking and squirting, they peered over at the newcomers, wondering who'd invaded their party.

"Hello," Clover smiled sheepishly. "I hope you don't mind us watching. That was the sexiest thing we've seen in a long time."

"Not at all," one of the native men said, peering at the three friends' pale bodies. "Where did you come from?"

"From different corners of the world," Tara nodded. "But we couldn't help stopping to admire your temple. Especially when we discovered we could bring you back to life..."

"Thank you," the second man said. "Our balls have been aching for *decades* waiting for us to be freed and allow us to spread our seed."

"Well, you seem to be spreading it *everywhere*," Clover

chuckled, glancing up at the dripping figures of the adjacent sculptures. "Perhaps you'd like to share it with some *other* willing partners?"

"Absolutely," the third man said, staring at Clover's and Tara's glistening pussies. "But what about your friend, here? It looks like he's got some juices of his *own* to share..."

"We were thinking of pairing up, two-on-one," Tara nodded. "That is, two of you joining up with Jessop, while Clover and I pair up with the third."

"That sounds interesting," the first man said, peering at Jessop's bobbing cock. "I've never done it with an *outsider* before. What do you say, Baasemi? Shall we give this boy an initiation into our culture?"

"If he's willing to open his mind, and a few *other* orifices..." the second man smiled.

"Alright," Tara nodded. "Why don't you three get comfortable while Clover and I see if we can find a way to keep your third partner entertained? I'm sure there's more than enough orifices to go around."

The third man stood up to join Clover and Tara, then the other two native men angled their bodies toward one another as they spread their legs further apart, signaling for Jessop to join them.

"Um...what did you have in *mind*, exactly?" Jessop said, approaching the two Sannyan men warily.

"Have you ever tried *stacking* your lingam with other men?" the second native man said, noticing Jessop's precum dripping from the tip of his cock, betraying his excitement at the prospect of hooking up with the hung tribesmen.

"Once or twice," Jessop nodded, squinting his eyes at their bobbing tools. "But never with anyone endowed with your size of equipment."

"It's just a matter of using the right *lubricant*," the first man said, grabbing hold of Jessop's dripping dick and pulling him toward them. He spread some of Jessop's precum over the tip of his instrument then he motioned for the newcomer to squat down over his hips, facing the second native man. Jessop did so carefully, and when the other man began to slide his hands over his shaft, he forgot that the man behind him was pointing his glans toward his flexing pucker. When he felt his sphincter stretching, he tensed up for a moment, then began to relax as the man in front caressed his tightening balls and stroked his throbbing hard-on.

"Unghh," Jessop moaned as he felt the man behind him begin to fill up his butthole while the tip of his cock stimulated the underside of his prostate gland. The feeling of being fucked by a foot-long cock as he was stimulated from the other side wasn't as bad as he imagined, and before long, he eased into a comfortable rhythm with the man positioned behind him while the man in front played with his tool, rubbing the tip of his own dripping instrument against Jessop's tight balls.

"That's a beautiful cock you have," the man in front said, stroking Jessop's erection harder while he bounced it playfully against Jessop's flexing abs. "I can't wait to see you spray your jelly over my stomach when you climax."

"Perhaps we can do it *together*," Jessop smiled, staring at the man's bigger erection bouncing up against his. "Rub your cock against mine while I feel your juice sliding down my pole."

"Yes," the second man said, rising up onto his knees to bring his organ level with Jessop's elevated hard-on resting over the other man's hips. "Your dick reminds me of mine in younger days..."

"Do your people always share your sexual energy so

freely?" Jessop groaned as his partner gripped the base of their joined cocks with two hands.

"We don't have any *restrictions,* if that's what you mean," the native man said, squeezing their two dicks harder together. "Young and old, men and women, similar sexes, it doesn't matter. We just enjoy the gift that Dheion has given us."

"It's too bad that *other* people aren't as open-minded as you Sannyans are," Jessop grunted, staring down at the other man's larger pole popping in and out of his hands. "There'd be a lot less jealousy and infighting if everybody was so accepting."

"Perhaps," the tribesman nodded as a deepening sex flush began to spread over his chest. "But we've paid the price from sheltering ourselves for so long. Our people were beginning to die off from our own self-absorption."

"We'll be happy to spread the word after we leave here," Jessop nodded. "We were just fortunate to find your temple hidden so far away in the wilderness."

"We'll see," the man moaned, pressing his balls harder up against Jessop's as the man behind plowed his ass harder. "There's a lot more of *us* than you. It might be better for us to seek out new partners while you continue to free our people. It seems you're the only ones who can free us from our bonds."

"I have a feeling that my friends will be more than happy to indulge," Jessop nodded, glancing over at Clover and Tara, who were kneeling together, facing the third native man's huge, upturned organ.

"The sooner, the better," the man panted, wrapping his legs around the ass of his partner while Jessop and he thrust their cocks upward together.

"I'm ready whenever you are," Jessop huffed, wrapping

his hands around the top of the tribesman's larger erection while he rubbed his own throbbing cock against his partner's pole. "I want to watch you spurt your juice all over my chest when we come together. This feels incredible–"

"Do you hear that, Baasemi?" the man said, glancing over at his fellow tribesman who was clutching the sides of Jessop's ass as he thrust his dick ever deeper into Jessop's bowels. "I think our friend is ready to spread his seed."

"See if you can catch some for the *women*," the other tribesman grunted. "We need to save every precious drop of their milk. Let's make this boy come harder than he has in a long time."

"I think he already *is*," the first man chuckled, staring down at the semen flowing through his fingers while he jerked Jessop's cock. "Something tells me we're about to have another geyser."

"Yes," Jessop hissed, squeezing the tip of the man's cock facing him harder as his muscles began to tighten up and a deep flush rolled over his face. "I can't hold it any longer. Let me watch your dick spurting together with mine."

Both men released their grip on the other's organs, then they arched their backs, pointing their dicks upward while they stared at their swelling crowns. When they both shot off, they erupted their juices upwards in a spring of glistening fluid, squirting against their own chests and their upturned chins while they grunted and convulsed together in pleasure. When the man in the rear felt Jessop's anus pulsing over his pole, he ejected his own semen deep inside Jessop's bowel, squeezing the other men's balls together to milk them dry. When they all finished shaking and climaxing, the man facing Jessop slid the palm of his hand over Jessop's dripping chest, spreading his seed over his own face and his lips, eager to share it with the next partner he'd have an opportunity to hook up with.

In the meantime, Jessop had been so lost in his *own* pleasure that his eyes bulged when he heard the sound of grunting and shifting bodies a few feet to his side. Now it was *his* turn to watch his friends share their juices with the other tribesman, who appeared only too eager to rub his oversize erection against their dripping pussies...

10

———

While the other three men lay down to enjoy the show unfolding next to them, they played with their dripping cocks as Clover and Tara became more aroused rubbing their pussies against the third tribesman's big erection.

"That's a work of *art*, wouldn't you agree, Tara?" Clover panted while her juices dripped down her slit over the man's bouncing balls.

"To say the least," Tara moaned as she curled her legs around Clover's ass. "I can only *dream* what it must feel like to have a cock that big."

"It would be kind of fun to have one like that to play with for a day or two," Clover nodded. "Can you imagine all the things we could do with a dick that size?"

"I'd probably just play with it by myself all day long," Tara chuckled. "Stroke it, suck it, *drink* it. No wonder these people never left the shelter of their little enclave all these years."

"Yes, it's a shame their leader froze them on the walls of

this temple," Clover said, beginning to feel an unusual new sensation emanating from her clit, growing harder at the top of her labia. "I wouldn't want to stop fucking for a *moment* if I was endowed like these tribespeople."

"Yeah," Tara huffed. "I think it feels even better screwing them from our side than being inside their own bodies."

"I know what you mean," Clover nodded, glancing between her legs at her swelling bulb. "It's almost like our *own* organs are growing to match their endowments..."

Tara peered down to look at her dilating nub and suddenly her eyes flit open.

"What the–?" she said, temporarily pulling her pussy away from the tribesman's upturned cock. "Are you seeing what *I'm* seeing?"

Clover paused her tribbing action for a moment and stared down at her puffy lips, barely believing what she was seeing.

"Is that what I *think* it is?" she said, staring at her expanding bean. "It almost looks like a–"

"A *cock!*" Tara gasped, watching her clit pressing outward and tilting upward toward her stomach.

"Holy shit!" Clover nodded, grabbing hold of her new appendage and caressing it softly. "It's enormous. And it feels–"

"Insane!" Tara nodded, squeezing and stroking her organ with increasing excitement. "You weren't kidding about larger being better."

"And the more I stroke it, the bigger it gets!" Clover said, wrapping both of her hands around her rising erection.

"Oh my God," Tara groaned, following Clover's lead and grabbing her flapping cock with two hands. "It feels even better when you rub the tip with one of your fingers..."

"Mmmft," Clover moaned as she rolled her thumb over the slippery crown. "I'm getting some serious *boy* envy. This is the greatest thing since–"

"Since that mysterious mage turned you into a hermaphrodite for a day?"

"Yes," Clover nodded, sliding her right hand lower between her legs to see if she still had any of her female parts. "And we've still got our *pussies*. I wonder what it feels like to–"

"*Fuck* each other?" Tara nodded. Then she turned to the tribesman, who was peering at them with a bemused expression while he played with his big cock.

"Do you mind if we take a few moments to try something different?" she said to the grinning native.

"Not in the least," the tribesman nodded. "Knock yourselves out. I'm sure the *rest* of us will enjoy it almost as much as you will."

He shifted his body away from the two women, then he sat next to the other three men who were now sitting hip-to-hip, watching the scene unfold. Tara paused for a moment, staring at Clover's upturned tool, with her mind running through all the things she wanted to do with her newly endowed partner.

"Who should go first?" she said, peering at Clover with a flushed face. "There's so many ways we could do this–"

"*You* go first," Clover said, raising up on her knees as she pressed her bouncing tool against Tara's belly. "Fuck me with that big dick of yours while I play with your tits. I want to feel you gushing inside me."

"Do you think it still *works* that way?" Tara said, widening her eyes.

"I don't see why not," Clover smiled. "I mean, these

people are all about spreading their seeds as much as possible."

"Thank God we found this place," Tara nodded. "I could stay here all *year*."

"It might take that long to finish freeing everyone," Clover chuckled. "Something tells me we're not going to get tired of it anytime soon."

"Sit on my cock then," Tara said, angling her throbbing erection towards Clover's dripping hole. "I want to play with your new dick while I fuck you hard."

"Mmm," Clover purred, positioning her slit over the tip of Tara's instrument and slowly lowering her body. "This feels sublime."

"Not as good as it does for *me*," Tara groaned when she felt Clover's instrument filling her cavity. "Just wait until you try this. This is even better than I imagined..."

"It's pretty fucking good from *my* end too," Clover grunted. "Your cock feels incredible inside my pussy."

Tara glanced down at Clover's big erection, watching it bounce against her stomach as she started to rock her hips.

"Does it feel even better when I do *this*?" she said, grabbing hold of Clover's hard-on with two hands, pumping her shaft while she pounded her ass.

"God, yes," Clover panted. "It's *more* than twice as good. It's almost like my cock is extending inside my pussy."

"Good," Tara huffed, feeling a new sensation building up inside her belly. "We can switch positions when I'm finished here. Right now, I feel like I'm going to explode."

"I feel it too," Clover nodded, glancing down at the tip of her new instrument, noticing it emitting copious amounts of fluid. "I'm not sure I can *wait* until you're finished. This feels way too good–"

"Let it go, baby," Tara hissed, clutching Clover's hips harder as the two women pressed their tits together, rocking their hips with newfound urgency. "We've got all day to explore the possibilities. I'm going to come so hard inside your burning pussy..."

"Oh God, Tara," Clover squealed as her face twisted up into a pained look of ecstasy. "Here it comes. *Fuckkkkkk...*"

When Tara saw her friend spraying her semen all over her tits while shaking in her arms, she lost all vestige of remaining control, tensing her body as she felt the pressure in her belly building to a busting point. When she felt her new dick pulsing hard inside Clover's pussy, she pulled her friend closer, reveling in their newfound pleasure while they shook their bodies together as the rest of the men rapidly stroked their erections, spraying their jizz over their quivering bodies. The two women's orgasm seemed to last forever, and when they finally finished climaxing together, they collapsed down next to the men, staring at their dripping tools.

"What *other* surprises are you tribespeople been keeping from us?" Tara panted, stroking their throbbing penises softly. "Because if you've got some other magic tricks up your sleeve, I can't wait to find out."

"I suppose you'll just have to keep working your way up the pyramid," the tribesman named Baasemi smiled. "The more of our tribe you free with your sexy bodies, the more pleasure I suspect you'll unlock from both sides."

"I don't know how much more of this I can take," Clover sighed, feeling utterly exhausted and spent. "I think I might need to take a breather before we explore our next pairing."

"Well, now that we've got two more *cocks* in the mix," Jessop chuckled, staring at his friends' new throbbing organs. "Something tells me you're not going to tire of unlocking the other secrets these Sannyans are protecting…"

*R*eady for more erotic chills and thrills? Read the next volume in Clover's Fantasy Adventures: *The Erotic Temple, Part 2.* Buy direct and save at victoriarusherotica. Or download from your favorite online bookstore here: retailer links.

Sometimes a hard man is good to find…

ALSO BY VICTORIA RUSH

Adult Fairytales:

The Enchanted Forest: An Erotic Fairytale

The Land of Giants: An Erotic Fairytale

The Dragon's Lair: An Erotic Fairytale

Witch's Brew: An Erotic Fairytale

The Mage's Spell: An Erotic Fairytale

The Mermaid Lagoon: An Erotic Fairytale

The Coven: An Erotic Fairytale

Rapunzel: An Erotic Fairytale

The Seven Dwarfs: An Erotic Fairytale

The Land of Mutants: An Erotic Fairytale

The Erotic Temple: A Sexy Fairytale (Coming Soon)

Erotica Themed Bundles:

Voyeur: Lesbian Erotica Bundle

Public Affairs: A Lesbian Anthology

Futa Fantasies: The Ladyboy Collection

Threesomes: The Lesbian Collection

Threesomes - Volume 2: The Lesbian Collection

First Time: A Lesbian Anthology

Hedonism: An Erotic Anthology

Switch Hitters: Bisexual Erotica

Taboo Erotica: The Lesbian Series

BDSM: The Lesbian Collection

Party Games: The Erotic Collection

Party Games 2: The Erotic Collection

All Girl 1: Lesbian Erotica Bundle

All Girl 2: Lesbian Erotica Bundle

All Girl 3: Lesbian Erotica Bundle

All Girl 4: Lesbian Erotica Bundle

Erotic Fairytale Bundles:

Clover's Fantasy Adventures: Books 1 - 5

Clover's Fantasy Adventures: Books 6 - 10

Erotic Fantasy:

Pirate's Bounty: A Time Travel Adventure

Wild West: A Time Travel Adventure

Private Riley: A Time Travel Adventure

Cleopatra's Secret: A Time Travel Adventure

Bounty Hunter 2125: A Time Travel Adventure

Ninja Assassin: A Time Travel Adventure

The 300: A Time Travel Adventure

Arabian Nights: An Erotic Fairytale (coming soon...)

Steamy Time Travel Bundles:

Riley's Time Travel Adventures: Books 1 - 5

Lesbian Erotica:

The Dinner Party: Lesbian Voyeur Erotica

The Darkroom: Bisexual Voyeur Erotica

Naked Yoga: Lesbian Transgender Erotica

Nude Cruise: Bisexual Voyeur Erotica

Rush Hour: Taboo Public Sex

The Girl Next Door: First Time Lesbian Erotic Romance

Girls' Camp: Lesbian Group Sex

Wet Dream: Ladyboy Fantasy Erotica

The Convent: Taboo Sex with a Nun

Sex Robot: A Dream Sex Machine

The Personal Trainer: Getting Pumped at the Gym

The Dominatrix: BDSM Lesbian Domination

Webcam Chat: Lesbian Online Sex

Paint Me: A Kinky Bodypainting Workshop

The Toy Party: Girls Sharing Sex Toys

The Costume Party: Strapping One On

Swedish Sauna: Lesbian Group Sex

The Therapist: Taboo Lesbian Erotica

Elevator Shaft: Bisexual Threesomes Erotica

Ladyboy: Lesbian Transgender Erotica

Peep Show: Lesbian Voyeur Erotica

The Dare: Public Sex Erotica

Maid Service: Lesbian Threesomes Erotica

The Hitchhiker: First Time Lesbian Erotica

The Housesitter: Spycam Lesbian Erotica

The Spa: Lesbian Group Orgy

Parlor Games: Blindfold Sex Party

The Exchange Student: First Time Lesbian Erotica

The Hostel: Bisexual Group Erotica

The Harem: Lesbian Erotic Romance

The Orient Express: Lesbian Voyeur Erotica

The First Lady: A Forbidden Lesbian Erotic Romance

The Slave: Lesbian BDSM Erotica

The Masseuse: Lesbian Sensuous Erotica

Too Close for Comfort: Lesbian Forbidden Erotica

Naked Twister: A Wild Party Game

Lexi: The Sex App (Lesbian Fantasy Erotica)

Call Girl: Lesbian Bisexual Threesomes Erotica

Circle Jill: Lesbian Masturbation Workshop

The Viewing Room: Masturbation Voyeur Erotica

Spin the Bottle: A Kinky Party Game

The Hair Salon: Lesbian Voyeur Erotica

Tribadism 1: Girls Only Sex Workshop

Tribadism 2: The Art of Scissoring

Tribadism 3: Threeway Hookups

The Kiss: A Game of Oral Sex

Pledge Week: Sorority Sisters

Carny Games 1: A Wild Sex Party

Carny Games 2: A Kinky Sex Party

Carny Games 3: An Erotic Sex Party

Dreamscape: An Artificial Reality Game

Glory Hole: Guess Who's On the Other Side

Joy Ride: A Late Night Erotic Bus Trip

The Blind Girl: An Erotic Romance(Coming Soon)

Lesbian Erotica Bundles:

Jade's Erotic Adventures: Books 1 - 5

Jade's Erotic Adventures: Books 6 - 10

Jade's Erotic Adventures: Books 11 - 15

Jade's Erotic Adventures: Books 16 - 20

Jade's Erotic Adventures: Books 21 - 25

Jade's Erotic Adventures: Books 26 - 30

Jade's Erotic Adventures: Books 31 - 35

Jade's Erotic Adventures: Books 36 - 40

Jade's Erotic Adventures: Books 41 - 45

Jade's Erotic Adventures: Books 46 - 50

Fifty Shades of Jade: Superbundle

Standalone Stories:

The Polynesian Girl: A Lesbian EroticRomance

FOLLOW VICTORIA RUSH:

Want to keep informed of my latest erotic book releases? Sign up for my newsletter and receive a FREE bonus book:

Spying on the neighbors just got a lot more interesting...